S0-BCX-993

CATS' TALES

FELINE FAIRY TALES
FROM
AROUND THE WORLD

Copyright for illustrations and layout © 1984 Nord-Süd Verlag,
Mönchaltorf, Switzerland
Copyright © for text by Eugen Diederichs Verlag, Köln, Germany
First published in Switzerland by Nord-Süd Verlag under the title
Märchenkatzen – Katzenmärchen
English text copyright © 1985 Anthea Bell
Copyright English language edition under the imprint
North-South Books © 1985 Rada Matija AG, Staefa, Switzerland

All rights reserved

First published in the United States, Great Britain, Canada,
Australia and New Zealand in 1985 by North-South Books,
an imprint of Rada Matija AG.

Distributed in the United States by
Holt, Rinehart and Winston, 383 Madison Avenue,
New York, New York, 10017.
Library of Congress Cataloging in Publication Data

Schmid, Eleonore.
  Cats' tales.

  Translation of: Marchen Katzen/Katzen Marchen.
  Summary: Twenty-one tales about cats from
different countries.   I. Tales.   [1. Folklore.
2. Cats – Fiction]   I. Title.
PZ8.1.S349Cat   1985   398.2'452974428   85-7185

ISBN 0-03-005732-9

Distributed in Great Britain by
Blackie and Son Ltd, Furnival House, 14–18 High Holborn,
London WC1V 6BX.
British Library Cataloguing in Publication Data

Cats' tales
  1. Cats – Folklore
  I. Schmid, Eleonore   II. Märchen Katzen, Katzen
  Märchen. *English*
  398.2'452974428   PZ10.3

ISBN 0-200-72874-1

Distributed in Canada by
Douglas & McIntyre Ltd., Toronto.
Canadian Cataloguing in Publication Data available in
Marc Record from National Library of Canada.
ISBN 0 88894 757 7

Distributed in Australia and New Zealand by
Buttercup Books Pty. Ltd., Melbourne.
ISBN 0 949447 14 5

Printed in Germany

Eleonore Schmid

CATS' TALES

English text by Anthea Bell

FELINE FAIRY TALES
FROM
AROUND THE WORLD

North-South Books
New York London Toronto Melbourne

CATS WILL BE CATS

Once upon a time there was a man who had a cat. As it was a very clever cat indeed, and nobody else had one like it, he gave it the name of Sky. One day a friend came to visit him. His friend was surprised by the cat's strange name, and asked, "What made you call your cat Sky?" – "Why," said the man, "my cat is so unique and precious that the mere word 'cat' is not right for it. Only the name of Sky suits it, for there is nothing more unique and precious than the sky." – "But cannot the clouds cover the sky?" asked his friend. "Well, yes," said the man, "so in that case I'll call it Cloud." – "But," said his friend, "the wind can drive the clouds away!" – "Very well, then I'll call it Wind!" – "Yet the city wall stands up to the wind." – "Then I'll call it City Wall." – "However, mice can dig their way through the city wall." – "Then I will call it Mouse." – "But the cat can catch mice." The man thought about that, and said, "Then I must call it Cat again." His friend clapped his hands and laughed, saying, "Don't you know the proverb that says cats will be cats?"

THE CAT IN THE PALACE

A poor man and his wife once had a cat. They had nothing to eat themselves, but they gave the cat food. They had nothing to drink themselves, but they gave the cat drink. Even so, the cat did not get what she liked best to eat: meat and liver. So she grew thin, until she was nothing but skin and bone, and almost dead. One day, as she was basking in the sun outside the couple's house, she saw the palace cats strolling along the wall of the great palace opposite. They were all as fat and round as eggs. She felt envious and longed to be one of them. "Oh," she thought, "how I wish I lived in the palace! If only I got what I like to eat, as those cats do, and not

what I don't like!" And then she thought, "Suppose I could climb the wall and get into the palace myself!" One day the cat saw her opportunity and jumped over the wall. Hearing the noise she made, all the palace guards, sentries, soldiers and police came running up. Frightened and confused, the cat ran hither and thither, and didn't know where to go. She bitterly regretted jumping the wall. In the end she climbed a tree. And as she looked down from the tree at the people below, she wept quietly to herself. "Oh," said she, "if I could get out of here, a corner in the old people's house would be Paradise!"

TWO CATS AND A LOAF

There were once two cats who found a loaf of bread, and they fell to quarreling about the best way to divide it.

Then along came the monkey. His mouth watered when he saw the loaf, and he thought to himself, "I'd like that bread." So he said, "If you can't agree, then let me help you. Nothing simpler! I'll weigh you out two fair shares." So saying, he was off.

He soon came back with a pair of scales, and began dividing the loaf. First he bit some off one half, then he bit some off the other half. And it always turned out that one half was heavier than the other. So he bit some more off one half, and then some more off the other half, and so on. And when there was almost none of the loaf left, the cats said, "Give us our loaf back and we'll divide the bread ourselves."

"Oh, I can't give you the rest of it back," said the monkey. "It's payment for all my hard work." And so saying, he stuffed the last bit into his mouth. Then the cats were sorry they had ever quarreled.

THE TALE OF THE CATS

Once upon a time there was a girl whose mother had died, and whose father had married again. But a few years later, her father died too, and so the girl lived all alone with her stepmother and a stepsister. However, her stepmother ill-treated her, and she got more blows than food, and more cross words than kind ones. The poor girl had to do all the housework by herself, while her stepsister idled her time away. One day her stepmother sent her out to gather some chicory. The girl walked on and on, but she couldn't find chicory anywhere. However, she saw a big cauliflower growing in a field. So she thought, "As I haven't found any chicory, I'll take this cauliflower home instead." But the cauliflower was unusually large. The girl tugged and tugged, and when at last she uprooted it she saw there was a deep shaft beneath it, with a little ladder going down into the ground. The girl climbed down to see what might be there. When she reached the bottom, she saw a house full of cats. They were all working busily away: one kitten was doing the washing, another kitten was fetching water from a well, one kitten was cooking the dinner, yet another kitten was washing the dishes, and the last kitten was baking bread. The girl asked one of the kittens to give her a broom, and she swept the house. Then she took some of the dirty laundry from another kitten and washed it until it was nice and clean. Then she helped the kitten who was fetching water, and last of all she put the bread in the oven.

By now it was noon, and all of a sudden in came a big cat, the mother of all these kittens, ringing a little bell, tingalingaling, and singing:

"If you've worked hard, you'll get your dinner,
but if you haven't you'll soon be thinner."

Then all the kittens came running up and said, "Oh, Mama, we all worked hard, but this girl worked much harder than we did."
"Well done," the cat told the girl. "Come along and have dinner with us!"
So they went into the house and sat down to dinner. The mother cat sat among the kittens and served the meal. She gave the girl meat, and macaroni, and roast chicken, but her children had nothing but beans. However, the girl was sorry for the little kittens, getting nothing but beans to eat, and she gave them some of all the good things the mother cat had given her.

When they rose from the table, the girl carried the dishes into the kitchen, washed them, and tidied the room. Then she went to the mother cat and said, "I must go now, dear Mrs Cat, or my stepmother will be anxious."
"Wait a moment," said the cat. "I'd like to give you something to take with you." And she led the girl into a room which was half full of fine linen, silken dresses and pretty little shoes, while the other half was full of coarse linen, plain dresses, stout shoes and scarves of wool. "Now choose what you would like," said the cat. The poor girl, who had no shoes to wear, asked for a pair of sturdy wooden clogs, and nothing more, but the cat said, "No, that won't do! You were good and kind to my kittens, and you worked so hard that I want to give you a handsome present!" And she chose a lovely silk dress for the girl, silk stockings, a scarf of fine needlework, and a pair of lovely satin slippers, and helped her to put the pretty things on. The girl was so overcome by the gift of these beautiful clothes that she couldn't find words to thank the cat.
However, the cat said, "When you climb up again, you'll find some holes in the wall; put your fingers in them and then raise your head!" With these words, she embraced the girl, and the girl climbed back up the ladder. Just before she reached the top of the shaft, she saw the holes and put her fingers in them, and when she took them out again there were rings on every finger, gold rings set with precious stones, each lovelier than the last. The girl raised her head, and a star fell on her brow. So she came home, dressed like a rich bride. When her stepmother saw her, she was so surprised that her mouth fell open.
"How did you come by those splendid things?" she asked her stepdaughter angrily. "Where did you steal them?"
"Oh, stepmother," said the girl, "I found a house all full of kittens, and helped them with their work, and that's where I was given these presents." And she told the whole story.
Next morning, her stepmother waited impatiently for dawn to come, so that she could send her own daughter to see the cats.
At last day broke, and the old woman told her daughter, "Get up, my dear, and go to see those cats. Then you'll get some beautiful jewels, just as your stepsister did."

"I don't want to," said she. "I don't feel like going out now, I haven't had my beauty sleep, and it's still so cold out of doors."

But her mother, who was greedy for the jewels, beat her and drove her out of the house. In a very bad temper, she went to the field, found the big cauliflower, pulled it up, muttering crossly, and climbed down the ladder. At the bottom of it she saw the kittens happily going about their work. But she made no move to help them. On the contrary, she pulled the first kitten's tail, pinched the second kitten's ear, and tugged at the third kitten's whiskers. One of the kittens was sewing, and she pulled the thread out of its needle, and when a kitten came in with water from the well, she knocked the bucket over. In short, she did nothing but torment the unhappy kittens and spoil their work. And so it went on all morning. The poor little kittens were mewing with pain and fright, but the girl didn't mind that a bit.

At last it was noon, and in came the mother cat with her bell, tingalingalaing, singing:

"If you've worked hard, you'll get your dinner,
but if you haven't you'll soon be thinner."

Then the kittens all came running up, saying, "Oh, Mama, we would have liked to do our work, but this girl came in and pulled our tails, and did all she could to disturb us. So we haven't done anything at all."

"Well, well," said the mother cat, "let's go and have dinner."

And they went into the house and sat down to dinner.

The cat gave the girl barley gruel, but the kittens had meat and noodles. However, the girl did not like her gruel, so she took the kittens' meat away from them. When they had finished dinner, the girl ignored the dirty dishes and told the mother cat, "Now, give me some clothes like the clothes you gave my stepsister!" So the cat took her into the room full of clothes and asked, "What do you want?"

"I want the best dress, the finest scarf, and the shoes with the highest heels!" said the girl.

"Well, get undressed, and I'll give you some clothes," said the cat. And she dressed the girl in an old skirt that was stiff with dirt, a filthy, ragged scarf, and coarse wooden clogs. Then she told the girl, "Off you go now, and before you climb out of the shaft, don't forget to put your fingers in the holes in the wall and raise your head!" But she need not have said that, for the girl already craved those gold rings set with precious stones. Without a word of farewell, the girl climbed the ladder and put her fingers in the holes, but when she drew them out, there was a worm curled round every finger, and she couldn't tear them off. And when she raised her head, a sausage fell into her mouth. She had to keep biting bits off it or she would have choked. When she came home, cold and dirty, looking uglier than a pig, her mother was so angry she fell down dead. And the girl herself soon died of fury because she had to keep biting bits off the sausage. So the good stepsister inherited the house, and before long a handsome young man came and married her and they lived happily ever after.

THE FOX AND THE CAT

It so happened that the cat met Master Fox in a wood one day, and thinking that the fox was clever and experienced and very well respected, the cat addressed him most politely. "Good day, dear Master Fox," said he, "how are you, and how do you do, and how are you managing in these hard times?" The proud fox looked the cat up and down, and it was quite a long while before he could make up his mind whether to answer the cat at all. At last he said, "Why, you wretched washer of whiskers, you foolish tabby, you hungry chaser of mice, what in the world are you thinking of? How dare you ask me how I am? What have *you* learned? Just how much can *you* do?" – "Oh, I can only do one thing," said the cat, modestly. "And what's that?" asked the fox. "When the dogs are after me, I can run up a tree and get away." – "Is that all?" said the fox. "Why, I can do over a hundred clever things, and I know a great many other tricks besides. I feel sorry for you, I really do. Come with me, and I'll teach you how to escape from dogs." But just then along came a huntsman, with four hounds. The cat jumped nimbly into a tree and climbed to the top of it, where the leaves and branches hid him. "Now let's see what *you* can do, Master Fox!" said the cat, but the hounds were on the fox and had him down. "Well, Master Fox," said the cat, "you can keep your hundred tricks! If you could have run up here along with me, you would have saved your life."

THE DOG AND THE CAT

The dog and the cat once said they would not serve their master unless he gave them meat to eat. Well, at first their master didn't like that, but when he saw they wouldn't serve him on any other terms, he gave in, and signed a contract with them. The cat took the contract away, up to the attic, and tied it to one of the rafters, where the mice found it and nibbled it all up.

After a while, the dog and the cat went to their master to ask for the meat he had promised them, and he said he would like to see the contract. But since neither the dog nor the cat could show it, he didn't give them as much as a sniff of their meat.

Then the dog and the cat quarreled. The dog told the cat to produce that contract, for without it they had no hope of any meat at all. But there was no way the cat could possibly show the contract, and so dog and cat have been deadly enemies ever since.

And since the cat, brave as he was, couldn't do the dog any harm, he took to chasing mice, because it was the mice who had eaten the contract.

THE TALE OF THE CAT WHO WAS WEAK WITH HUNGER

Once upon a time there was a tom cat who had stolen a great many things from a venerable monk. One day, when the cat was running away with a string of prayer beads in his mouth, the monk chased him, caught him just as he was about to slip into his hole, and pulled his tail so hard that it came off.

As a result, the cat fell sick, and while he lay growing thin and weak with hunger, he thought of a trick. He put the string of prayer beads around his neck, and sat in a passage, looking harmless.

A mouse saw him there, and turned to run away in fright, but the cat said, "Have no fear, my child! As I am a monastic cat, bound by vows and duties, I take no life and commit no sins. Oh, if only you mice would turn to religion, like me!"

These remarks converted the mouse, who repeated them to his own people. He called a number of them together, and they listened to the cat preaching a sermon.

Then the cat said, "Now that you have all heard my sermon, I want you to walk around me in single file, confessing your faith, and then off you go to your own holes!"

And every time he said these words after his sermon, and made the mice walk past him in single file, he would catch the mouse at the end of the line and eat it. When several mice had been eaten, and the others were beginning to suspect something, they discussed the matter together and wondered if the cat really did take no life.

When they next heard one of his sermons, they asked the cat, "Master, what do you generally eat?" And the cat said, "Well, I usually live on dried leaves and herbs."

So a mouse called Number One, who was used to looking after himself, gathered all the mice together, and told them what to do.

"Get a little bell on a ribbon from some human house," said he. "We will hang this bell around the cat's neck, and then, if you hear the sound of it while we are leaving after hearing his sermon, you must all look behind you!"

So they found a bell, and when it was time to assemble and hear the cat's sermon, they said, "We would like to give our master this ornament!" And they hung the bell around the cat's neck. But when they had heard the sermon, and they were all setting off for home, they heard the bell ring, just as they had expected, and turned to look back. The cat had pounced on a mouse and was busy eating it. So the mouse Number One said, "Our master's belly has grown nice and fat, but there's fewer of us poor mice than there used to be. I think these sermons are a snare and a deception."

At these words from their leader, the mice turned tail, scattered and ran home to their own holes.

Ever since that day no mouse will ever trust a cat.

THE TIGER AND THE CAT

A farmer was plowing his land outside a village. His cat had come along too, and while the man and his oxen were plowing, the cat went chasing butterflies and grasshoppers on the outskirts of the forest. Now at that time the tiger was prowling the forest, and he was very much surprised when he saw the cat from afar. "Little brother," said the tiger, "you are obviously one of our family, but why are you so small?" The cunning cat pretended to be very miserable, and replied, "Oh, great lord, Tsar of all the animals, if only you knew how hard it is living with humans!"

"Who dares oppress you? Show me the man, and I'll call him to account!" said the tiger.

The cat led the tiger to the farmer following his plow. "Now then, man," said the tiger, "why are you so hard on my little brother that he can't even grow? What has he ever done to harm you? I'm ready to fight you for his sake."

"Oh, by all means," said the farmer, "only I've left my strength at home. I'll just go and fetch it, and then we can fight." – "Very well," said the tiger, "off you go,

and I'll wait for you." – "But suppose you are deceiving me, and you go off somewhere else, and then I've had my trouble for nothing?" said the farmer. "Let me tie you to this tree with a rope while I run home to the village, and I'll come back with my strength, and then we can fight each other."

"Very well," agreed the tiger.

So the farmer tied him to a tree with a thick rope, went off into the forest, cut himself a sturdy cudgel from an ash tree, and came back again. "Here's my strength!" said he, and he began thrashing the tiger. The tiger roared, all heaven and earth pitied him, but the man didn't stop until he had beaten him to a pulp. Then he untied him and said, "You just keep out of my business! Off you go, and whenever you think of boasting, don't forget to think of me too!"

The tiger dragged himself away, more dead than alive, and when he saw the cat he sighed heavily and said, groaning, "Little brother, you're a very fine fellow! How did you ever manage to grow to that size in the power of such a terrible wild beast?"

WHY DOG AND CAT ARE ENEMIES

A man and his wife once had a golden ring. Now this ring had special powers and whoever owned it would always have enough to live on. However, they didn't know that, and one day they sold the ring cheap. No sooner was it out of the house than they became poorer and poorer, until they didn't know where to get enough to eat. They had a dog and a cat who were starving too. The dog and the cat talked to each other, wondering how they could help the couple regain their good fortune. At last the dog thought of a way. "They must have that ring back," he told the cat. And the cat said, "But the ring is shut up in a box where no one can get at it."

"You go and catch a mouse," said the dog, "and the mouse can gnaw its way through the box and take the ring. Tell it that if it doesn't, you will kill it, and then we'll have no trouble."

The cat liked this idea, so she caught a mouse, and set off with it for the house where the box was, followed by the dog. Then they came to a great river. Since the cat couldn't swim, the dog took her on his back and swam over the water. The cat carried the mouse to the house with the box in it, the mouse gnawed a hole in the box and took out the ring, the cat took the ring in her mouth and went back to the river, where the dog was waiting, and he carried her across once more. Then they started home together, taking the lucky ring to their master and his wife.

Since the cat could scamper straight across the rooftops while the dog had to stay on the ground, and walk round all obstacles, she arrived home well before the dog, and gave her master the ring.

"What a good creature our cat is!" said the man to his wife. "We will always give her plenty to eat, and care for her like our own child."

When at last the dog arrived, they beat him and were angry with him for not helping to bring the ring home. But the cat just sat there purring, and said nothing. So the dog was angry with the cat for cheating him of his reward, and whenever he saw her he chased her and tried to catch her.

And from that day forward, dog and cat have been enemies.

THE POOR MILLER'S MAN AND THE LITTLE CAT

There was once an old miller who lived in his mill. He had neither wife nor children, but he had three men to serve him. One day, when these three men had been with him several years, he told them, "I am old, and I plan to give up work and sit by the fire. Go out into the world, and I will give my mill to the man who brings me the best horse. In return, the man who gets the mill is to care for me to the end of my days."

Well, the third and youngest of the miller's men was only a boy, and the others thought him a simpleton, and didn't want him to have the mill. And in the end he didn't want it either. But all three set out together, and when they were past the village the other two told stupid Hans, "You might as well stay here, because you'll never find a horse in all your days." However, Hans went on with them, and when night fell they came to a cave and lay down in it to sleep. The two clever miller's men waited until Hans was asleep; then they rose and set off again, leaving Hans lying there. They thought they had done a very cunning thing – ah, but no good would come of it!

When the sun rose, Hans awoke, and found himself lying in a deep cave. He looked around, and said, "Where can I be?" So then he got up and made his way out of the cave. He walked away into the forest, thinking, "Here I am, all alone, and how will I ever get a horse?" As he was walking along, lost in thought, he met a little spotted cat. "Where are you going, Hans?" asked the cat, in friendly tones. "Oh," said Hans, "you couldn't help me." – "I know what it is you want," said the little cat, "you want a fine horse. Come and serve me faithfully for seven years, and I will give you a finer horse than you ever saw in your life." – "Why, this is a strange cat," thought Hans, "but I might as well see if she is telling the truth."

So the cat took him back to her enchanted castle, which was full of little cats that served her. They scurried up and down the stairs and were cheerful and merry. When they sat down to supper in the evening, three of the cats made music: one played the double bass, another played the fiddle, and the third puffed out its cheeks and blew the trumpet. After supper, the table was taken away, and the cat said, "Come and dance with me, Hans." – "No," said Hans, "I'm not dancing with a cat, for I never did such a thing before." – "Well, put him to bed," she told the little cats. So one of them lit the way to his bedroom, one took off his shoes and

one took off his stockings, and last of all one of them blew out the candle. Next morning they came back and helped him to rise: one of them put his stockings on, one of them tied his garters, one of them brought his shoes, one of them washed him, and one dried his face with its tail. "How nice and soft that feels," said Hans. However, he had to serve their mistress himself, chopping wood every day. He had a silver axe and a silver wedge and saw, and his mallet was made of copper. So Hans chopped wood, and lived in the castle, where he had good food and drink, but he never saw anyone except the little cat and her servants. One day she told him, "Go and mow my meadow and make hay of the grass," and she gave him a silver scythe and a golden whetstone, and told him to make sure he brought it all home again. So Hans did as she said, and when he had finished his work he brought home the scythe, the whetstone and the hay, and asked if she would give him his payment now. "No," said the cat, "I have another task for you. Here are silver timbers, a carpenter's axe and all the other tools you need, all made of silver, and I want you to build me a little house." So Hans built the little house, and said he had done all his work now, but still he had no horse. However, the seven years had passed like six months. The cat asked if he would like to see her horses. "Yes, indeed," said Hans. Then she opened the door of the little house, and there were twelve horses standing inside, and very proud horses they were, their coats so smooth and shiny that his heart rejoiced. The cat gave Hans food and drink, and said, "Go home now; your horse will not come with you, but I will follow bringing it in three days' time." So Hans set off, and she told him the way to the mill. She had not even given him a new coat, so he had to wear the ragged old clothes he had brought with him, though they had grown too small in those seven years.

When he got home the two other miller's men were back too, each with his horse, but one horse was blind and the other lame. "Where's your horse, Hans?" they cried. "It's coming in three days' time," he said. They laughed, and said, "Why, Hans, where do you suppose you're getting a horse? That'll be the day!" Hans went into the mill, but the miller said he couldn't sit at table with them, because he looked so tattered and torn, he would put them to shame if anyone happened to call. So they gave him a morsel of food, and when night

came the other two would not let him have a bed. He had to lie on harsh straw with the geese in their pen. When he woke in the morning, the three days were up, and along came a coach with six horses, and very fine horses they were!

A servant was leading a seventh, and that was for the poor miller. A beautiful princess got out of the coach and went into the mill. The princess was the little spotted cat that Hans had served for seven years. She asked the miller where the youngest miller's man was. "Oh," said the miller, "we can't have him in the mill with us, because he's so tattered and torn. He is out with the geese in their pen." So the princess told them to go and fetch him.

Hans was fetched, and he had to hold his clothes together to cover him. But then the servant unpacked some magnificent garments, and washed him and dressed him, and when he was ready no king could have looked finer. Then the princess asked to see the horses the other miller's men had brought home, one of which was blind and the other lame. Next she told the servant to bring in the seventh horse, and when the miller saw it, he said no horse like that had ever set foot in his yard before. "Well, it is for the third miller's man," said she. "Then he must have the mill," said the miller. But the princess said no. She told the miller to keep the horse, and to keep his mill as well, and she took faithful Hans and placed him in her coach and drove away with him. First they went to the little house he had built with silver tools, and it had turned into a great castle, with everything in it made of silver and gold, and then she married him, and he was rich, so rich that he need never want for anything in his life. So let no one say that a simpleton can never make good!

THE KING OF THE CATS

One winter's evening the sexton's wife was sitting by the fireside with her big black cat, Old Tom, on the other side. Both were half asleep and were waiting for the master to come home. They waited and they waited, but still he didn't come, until at last he came rushing in, calling out, "Who's Tommy Tildrum?" in such a wild way that both his wife and his cat stared at him.

"Why, what's the matter?" said his wife, "and why do you want to know who Tommy Tildrum is?" – "Oh, I've had such an adventure. I was digging away at old Mr Fordyce's grave when I suppose I must have dropped asleep, and only woke up by hearing a cat's meow." – "Meow!" said Old Tom in answer. "Yes, just like that! So I looked over the edge of the grave, and what do you think I saw?"

"Now, how can I tell?" said the sexton's wife. "Why, nine black cats all like our friend Tom here, all with a white spot on their chests. And what do you think they were carrying? Why, a small coffin covered with a black velvet pall, and on the pall was a small crown made of gold, and at every third step they took they cried all together, meow –"

"Meow!" said old Tom again.

"Yes, just like that!" said the sexton. "And as they came nearer and nearer to me I could see them more distinctly, because their eyes shone out with a sort of green light. Well, they all came towards me, eight of them carrying the coffin, and the biggest cat of all walking in front for all the world like – but look at our Tom, how he's looking at me. You'd think he knew all I was saying."

"Go on, go on," said his wife, "never mind Old Tom."

"Well, as I was a-saying, they came towards me slowly and solemnly, and at every third step crying all together, meow –"

"Meow!" said Old Tom again. "Yes, just like that, until they came and stood right opposite Mr Fordyce's grave, where I was, when they all stood still and looked straight at me. I did feel queer, that I did! But look at Old Tom; he's looking at me just like they did."

"Go on, go on," said his wife, "never mind Old Tom."

– "Where was I? Oh, they all stood still looking at me, when the one that wasn't carrying the coffin came forward and, staring straight at me, said to me – yes, I tell 'ee, *said* to me, with a squeaky voice, 'Tell Tom Tildrum that Tim Toldrum's dead,' and that's why I

asked you if you knew who Tom Tildrum was, for how can I tell Tom Tildrum Tim Toldrum's dead if I don't know who Tom Tildrum is?"

"Look at Old Tom, look at Old Tom!" screamed his wife. And well he might look, for Tom was swelling and Tom was staring, and at last Tom shrieked out, "What – old Tim dead! Then I'm the King of the Cats!" and rushed up the chimney and was never more seen.

THE CAT AND THE MOUSE

Once upon a time there was a man who found the mice were wreaking havoc in his pantry. So he got a cat, to rid him of those mice. Now one of the mice was very big, much stronger than the others, and when he saw what had happened he found a chance to speak to the cat from a place of safety, and told her, "I know that your master has given you orders to kill me and my friends, and so get rid of us. I am very pleased to meet you, and I'd like to be in your good graces, and live in peace and friendship with you." To which the cat replied, "I am wonderfully pleased to meet you too, and I would be delighted if you would honor me with your friendship. There's nothing I would like better than to live with you in peace and friendship, but I had better not promise what I can't perform. For you see, most noble mouse, my master has made me keeper of his house, to stop you and your kin from doing any more damage. If I were to spare you, he would call me a bad cat! So you must either stop stealing from my master, or leave the house and find yourself some other pleasant place to live. And don't blame me if you get hurt."

The mouse said, "I have asked you civilly, and I will ask you again, to forgive me my boldness and grant me your friendship."

"Oh, I like you well enough," said the cat, "but how am I to reconcile friendship with you and my duty, considering all the damage your comrades have done to my master's property? If I let you live, then he'll kill me, and that's no good. So I give you three days' grace to look about for another home." The mouse replied, "It would be hard for me to leave this place, I'll take care not to come too close to you, and stay as long as I like." Well, the cat gave the mouse three days' grace, as she had promised, and the mouse began to feel safe, and acted as if there were no cat in the place at all. But when the three days were up, and the mouse strolled out of his hole without a care in the world, there was the cat, lying in wait in a corner of the larder, and she pounced, and caught the mouse, and ate him all up.

THE HYENA AND THE WILD CAT

The hyena had a cub, and it died. The wild cat had a kitten, and it died. The wild cat could not bear to live in that part of the country any more, and the hyena could not bear to live there either. So they both went looking for a better place to live.

When the hyena had found a place, he said, "So far, so good. I will come at break of day tomorrow and pull up the grass."

By chance, the wild cat found the same place. He liked the spot, pulled up the grass, and went away again. Next morning the hyena came back. "Oh, what a fine place!" he cried. "I was going to pull up the grass, and it's pulled itself up." He took possession of the place, swept the ground, and went away again.

Then the wild cat came back again. "Oh, what a fine place!" he cried. "I was going to sweep the ground, and the ground has swept itself." He cut down a couple of trees, left them lying there and went away again.

Then the hyena came back, rammed the tree trunks into the ground and went off to sleep.

Then the wild cat came back. "The trunks have rammed themselves into the ground," he said, and he cut some bamboo canes and laid them ready.

The hyena came back again and fastened the bamboos to the trunks.

The wild cat came back again. "Aha," he cried, "the bamboo has fastened itself to the trunks," and he thatched the house with grass.

"How can this be?" cried the hyena, when he came back again. "The roof is on the house already." He divided the house in two; he kept one room for himself and left the other for his wife.

Then the wild cat came back. "Excellent," said he, "the house is divided in two already. I'll have this room for myself and give the other to my wife. I will bring my belongings in five days' time and settle here." And the hyena made the same plans.

On the fifth day, along came the wild cat, with his wife and his belongings. And along came the hyena with his own wife and belongings as well.

The hyena moved into one room, the wild cat moved into the other. Each of them thought he was alone in the house. Suddenly, at the same moment, each of them broke something. "Who's breaking something in the next room?" they both asked. And they both ran away. They ran as far as from Keta to Amutino, and then they met.

"What are you doing here, Hyena?" asked the wild cat.

"I built a house," said the hyena, "and something, I don't know what, has driven me out."

"The same thing happened to me," said the wild cat.

"I felled some trees, and the trees rammed themselves into the ground," said the hyena.

"I found a fine place, and when I came back to pull up the grass, it had pulled itself up," said the wild cat.

Then the wild cat and the hyena ran away from each other in confusion. And they have never dared to look each other in the eye from that day to this.

THE WHITE CAT

There was once a king who had three sons. One of them was proud, one of them was bad, and the other was very good, far too good, for his goodness was often abused.

Well, the king was old; he had a large kingdom and could scarcely rule it any more. So he thought: I will have one of my sons to help me and sit beside me on the throne. However, if I choose the eldest, he is so proud that he will be haughty with the people, and much injustice will be done. If I choose the second, who is bad, he will oppress the people, and that will be even worse. And if I choose the youngest, the other two won't give me a moment's peace. What am I to do? He thought and he thought, and when evening came he called his three sons to him and said he was old now, and needed someone to help him, and – "The kingdom is mine!" said the first. "Yours?" said the king. "No, you are too proud!" – "As for me, I'm bold!" said the second. "Yes, but you are bad." And the third said nothing. "What about you?" asked the king. "Oh, I wouldn't mind ruling, but I'd like everyone to be happy." – "That's what I thought you'd say," said the king. "Well, listen to me, my sons: I give you three years, three months, three weeks, three days and three hours, and whichever of you brings me home the finest fabric in the world will get my kingdom."

So the three agreed to that. The two elder princes thought: we've nothing to fear from our little brother! And off they went, in different directions. The youngest liked to go hunting, and while he was good he was a little careless and willing to let things be, and he thought: with three years, and as many months and weeks and days and hours, I've plenty of time. So he traveled from land to land, went hunting and came back to his lodgings at night, but he never thought of what he had to do.

So one evening he had been out hunting and came into a forest, when there was a terrible storm. Lightning flashed, and it began to rain so hard that he lost his way. So he sat down under a tree and fell asleep. However, he couldn't sleep for long, for he heard the wolves howling and the foxes calling and the owls hooting, so that he could get no rest. And he felt a strange fear. Well, he stood up, and away in the distance he saw a light. So he thought: I'll go toward that light. And he went toward the light, and the closer he came to it the greater the light seemed.

Then, all of a sudden, he found himself at the gate of a great castle. But the gate was closed. So he raised the knocker and banged on the gate. Slowly it opened and four hands came out. Four hands, and that was all. Two of the hands took him by one shoulder, and the other two hands by the other shoulder. And they led him down a wide passage and up a magnificent white marble staircase, and opened the doors of a great hall. Inside the hall, a fire was burning on an open hearth, and a complete suit of knightly clothing lay beside the hearth. The hands took him, sat him down on a chair, undressed him and dried him and took his wet clothing away, and dressed him as a knight. The four hands did all this, but never a word was spoken. And when he was fully clothed again, they took him by the shoulders and led him down the stairs again, opened a door, and led him into a great dining room, where the table was laid for two. They made him sit down on one of the two chairs. There was a roast mouse on a plate at the place opposite. But still he heard no sound, and there was nothing to be seen but those hands, just four hands. Then all at once the door opened, and in came a large white cat, but she didn't walk on all fours, she walked on her hind legs, and she was as tall as a woman. She had a black veil and a crown upon her head, and a wide blue ribbon with an noble order on it over her breast. And there were two great black tom cats with her, as guards. One carried a drawn sword, and the other bore the end of her veil.

She made him a curtsey, and said, "Welcome to my castle. I am glad to see a human being, after so many years and days. Please sit down!" So he sat down, and she said something to the two guards, who went out and came back with a wonderful meal for him, while the cat ate her mouse. Then she asked him where he came from, and who he was. He had been frightened at first, but the cat was so friendly that he had no fears now. Then she asked whether he liked hunting. "Why, yes!" Then he could go hunting tomorrow, said she, he had only to look behind the castle and he would find a horse there, a wooden horse to take him to the hunting ground. And the horse would bring him home again at nightfall. Sure enough, when he rose and went out next morning, there was a wooden horse such as children use in play. He mounted the horse, and no sooner was he on it than a whole flock of hands came following after them. One pair carried his gun, and another his

rucksack, and another his provisions. So they stayed out hunting all day long, and by the time they went home in the evening they had a fine bag of game. So he stayed at the castle, and the time passed quickly, and he quite forgot what he had to do.

However, one day when he had just risen, he happened to look at the calendar, and he saw that he had only three months left before he was to be home: three months, three weeks and three days. So he began to feel dejected, and did not go hunting anymore. The white cat asked him what was wrong. Then he admitted that he had not told her his full story, and he was a king's son. His father, he said, had given him three years, three months, three weeks, three days and three hours to bring home the finest fabric in the world, and now he had only three months, three weeks and three days left, and his own country was very far away. So he had no time to go hunting, if he was to get home. Oh, said the cat, he needn't worry about that. She gave the hands an order, and they brought her a walnut. She told him to take the nut and open it. But he must be careful, she said, only to take the two halves of the nutshell apart and not crack it. So he took the walnut and opened it, and there was a cherrystone inside. He wasn't to crack the cherrystone either, but twist it open, for that was how it was made. So he twisted the cherrystone open, and out came a wonderful fabric, lovely and shining as the sun, and finer than the finest cobweb. The cherrystone contained length upon length of this fine fabric. He must take the fabric home, said the cat, and if he set off a day before the appointed hour, that would be time enough. She would make sure, said she, that he was home in time. Well, now he had the fabric he was happy, and he stayed on at the castle.

The evening before he was to go home, she said that when he rose in the morning he was to mount the wooden horse again and cry, "Gee up!" But he must hold tight to the horse and close his eyes, for it would go so fast that he might fall off if he didn't.

Well, he took his walnut and went down the stairs, and along came the horse. And no sooner had he cried, "Gee up!" than the horse took a great leap and went speeding over hill and dale, over rivers and seas. And in no time at all, there he was outside his father's castle. His brothers were back too. Their father was pleased to see them, and summoned the eldest son. He had brought home a fabric so fine that he could hold length upon length of it on the palm of his hand. "Now," said he, "the kingdom's mine!" – "Wait, if you please," said his father. The second son took a tobacco tin out of his pocket, and he pulled length upon endless length of fabric out of that tobacco tin. "What about you?" the king asked the youngest son. So he brought out his walnut, opened the two halves of its shell, took out the cherrystone, and drew his fabric out of it. Then his father said, "I think you must agree he has brought the finest fabric, so the kingdom is his." – "No," said the others, "we don't agree, let's have another task!" – "Very well," said their father, "another task it is, but this time I'm giving you only three months, three weeks, three days and three hours, and never mind the three years. And you must bring me home the smallest dog you can find."

So off they went again. The youngest son took his horse and rode back to the white cat's castle, and this time he told her the whole story. Oh, said she, he needn't worry about that. So he stayed at the castle again, went out hunting, and let time pass by until the day was near for him to go home, and then the day came. The evening before, the cat gave him a tassel, such as you might find on a sofa, and she told him to listen to it. So he held the tassel to his ear, and listened, and heard a faint little, "Woof, woof!" inside. Then he unscrewed the top of the tassel, and out jumped a dog. The dog was so small that it could stand with all four paws on his thumb. "Now, off you go," said the white cat, "take your wooden horse again and be off." And once more he was home again in no time at all. Well, the eldest brother had brought a dog small enough to fit into his coat pocket. And the second had brought a dog so small that he could make it jump about on a book. Our young prince took out his tassel, unscrewed the top of it, and his dog was jumping about on his thumb. So the king said, "Well, really, there's nothing for it, you must have the kingdom!" However, the others wouldn't agree to that, and they said, "Oh, well, anybody can bring you a length of fine fabric or a little dog, can't they?"

"Then why couldn't you?" said the king. "Oh, very well, but this is the last task," he added. The eldest son said, "But let me say what we are to bring you. This time, whoever brings home the fairest bride will win! That's a more difficult task than bringing you lengths of fabric or dogs." So they all agreed, and the elder princes went away again.

The youngest took his horse and rode off too, taking most of his clothes with him. When he got back to the white cat, he told her that this time he was planning to stay. For this time, said he, he had only three weeks, three days and three hours, and this time... Why, she asked, didn't he want to go home again? He wasn't going home, he said, for if he did the kingdom would be given to one of his brothers, and either of them would oppress their subjects, and he wouldn't care for that, he would rather stay in the forest with her. But what, said the cat, must he take home now? Oh, she couldn't help with that! Let him tell her, all the same, said she. Well, she had to press him and press him until at last he told her. "I must bring home the fairest bride of all."

"Is that all?" said she. And she turned to the black tom cat with the sword and said, "Have you sharpened the blade well?"

"Yes," said the black cat. So she gave the young prince the sword and said, "Now you must cut my head off." No, said he, she had been so good to him, he could never do such a thing. But she begged him so hard and so fervently that at last he took the sword and cut off her head. And when he had cut her head off the castle rang with cries of joy. However, when he brought down the sword he had covered his eyes with his left hand, so as not to see her blood flowing.

When he looked, the white cat and the black cat were gone. Suddenly the doors opened, and in came a tall and beautiful young woman with a crown on her head. She went up to him and told him not to grieve, for he had set her free. She was the white cat, she said, and a witch had cast a spell upon her and all her servants many years ago. The witch had taken away the servants' bodies, leaving them with nothing but their hands, and as for herself, she had been turned into a white cat, and her chief ministers, who were standing by her side, were changed into black cats. Now he had broken the spell, and she gave him not only her hand but her kingdom too.

So they set off and came home in time, and the youngest prince's bride was the fairest of all.

As for the other two brothers, they were so angry they could have died of it. But the young prince told them to lay aside their pride and their badness, and share their father's kingdom between them. For he had his wife's kingdom now, and that was all the kingdom he needed.

THE CAT AND THE SIMPLETON

Once upon a time there was a man who had three sons. Two of the sons were clever, but one was stupid. The father fell sick, and had no hope of recovery. Before he died, he divided his goods equally between his two clever sons. When the stupid son saw that his father had left nothing for him, he began to weep and wail. "Why did you leave me out, father?" he asked. The old man thought, and then said, "Well, my son, I've left all that I own between your elder brothers, except for my cat and my stove, but you can have those." The simpleton thanked him, and then the father died.

No sooner had they buried him than the clever brothers took the simpleton by the scruff of his neck and flung him and the cat out. "Go and earn your own bread," said they, "we're not feeding any idlers!" The simpleton went off and lay down on the ashes next to the stove, with the cat under his head to keep him warm. There he lay for a long, long time, and then he felt hungry and shouted, "I want something to eat, I want something to eat!" And picking up the cat, he said, "I'll eat you." – "Oh, wait a minute," said the cat, "don't eat me, and I'll fetch you some food." So off went the cat, climbing over the rooftops and sniffing about for something to eat.

He came back with a sausage and gave it to the simpleton. No sooner had the simpleton eaten his fill than he shouted, "I want to get married!" However, there was nothing the cat could do about that, so the simpleton went on shouting until he wanted something else to eat. This went on, day after day: when he was hungry he shouted, "I want something to eat!" and when he had eaten his fill he shouted, "I want to get married!" In the end he began to beat the cat, and the cat thought, "Well, I'll have to get him married, but he doesn't look very attractive all covered with ashes. Who'd want him for a husband?"

The cat thought about it for a long time, and at last he had an idea.

He found a heap of leftover tailor's scraps, collected little patches and made the simpleton some clothes. Then he found a heap of leftover cobbler's scraps, collected little bits of leather and an end of cobbler's thread, and made a pair of boots. He gave the simpleton something to eat, washed him, and dressed him in his new clothes. As everyone knows, clothes make the man, and now the simpleton looked so handsome that he could have come before the king's daughter herself,

and the cat never tired of gazing at him. "Now we'll go up to the manor house a-wooing," said the cat. "Call yourself Lord Ashblower, for you used to lie among the ashes, sit there like a grand gentleman and don't say a word, hold up your head and don't look down at yourself." So they went up to the big, grand manor house. When they arrived, the lord of the manor was astonished to meet a cat who could talk, but not nearly as astonished as the young lady, his daughter. However, when the cat told them how great Lord Ashblower's property was, and how he wanted to marry the young lady, she immediately consented to be his bride. But her parents wanted to know if all the cat had told them about Lord Ashblower's property was true, and they decided to visit him before the wedding. They summoned their friends, put the simpleton in a coach, and off they all drove, with the cat running on ahead of them.

They went on, and they went on, and they came to the land of the mountain cave. The herdsmen there were looking after a great herd of cows. "Whose herdsmen are you?" the cat asked them. "We serve the dragon of the mountain cave." "Don't say you are the dragon's herdsmen, say you serve Lord Ashblower, for Grom and Perun are roaring along the road after me, and if you don't say that they will kill you." Well, when the lord of the manor asked whose herdsmen they were, they did as the cat had told them. Then the cat met the grooms of the dragon of the mountain cave, put terror in their hearts too with his tale of Grom and Perun, and told them to say they were Lord Ashblower's grooms. So they answered the lord of the manor in just the same way. By now the young lady's father was all puffed up with pride to think he would have such a rich gentleman for his son-in-law. At last the cat came to the dragon's court, and he cried, "Lord Dragon, quick, hide somewhere, for Grom and Perun are flying after me to kill you and crush you to dust." Well, of course the dragon was horribly frightened of Grom and Perun. "Where can I hide?" said he. There was a great hollow lime tree growing in the middle of the courtyard. "Quick, climb inside the hollow tree!" said the cat. The dragon was so scared that he suspected nothing, and was stupid enough to get inside the tree. That was all the cat wanted: he boarded up the way into the hollow trunk and covered it over with clay. Then he told the dragon's servants, "Don't say you serve the dragon of the mountain cave, if you value your lives! Say you serve Lord Ashblower, for Grom and Perun are flying along after me, and if you don't say that they will smash you and crush you and stamp you into the ground like sour apples." So all the servants were dreadfully scared.

Meanwhile, the wedding guests came driving into the courtyard, and they were amazed to see so fine and magnificently furnished a place. The servants hurried to meet them and led the young couple into the dragon's halls. Then the wedding was held, and a very merry wedding it was. So now the simpleton was lord of the dragon's court. And though it's true that he was no cleverer than he had been before – well, why need a rich man be clever? When the Lord God gives a man high rank, He gives him understanding too.

THE DANGEROUS CAT

Somewhere or other there lived an old man who had nothing to eat and nothing to drink. So he went off into deserts and wildernesses. He put his only possession, a cat named Mustapha, into a sack and took it with him. Soon he came to a country where there were no cats at all. Instead, there were a great many mice. Wishing to be a guest in one of the houses there, he sat down to eat bread.

Then along came ten men, with sticks in their hands. The old man with the cat was afraid, and said to himself in alarm, "They are going to beat me because I'm eating bread." However, they said, "We've brought these

sticks along for the mice, not you." At that the old man let the cat's head look out of the sack. Now it was the turn of the men to be afraid, for they had never seen such an animal before. However, no sooner did the cat see the mice than he jumped out of the sack and killed ten of them. Then he went back to his master.

This amazing and terrible news was immediately brought to the king. "The cat's killed ten!" The king sent for the old man, who wished him good day, and they drank a cup of coffee. Then he took his cat, Mustapha, out of the sack. "Old man," said the king, "will you sell us Lord Mustapha of the long whiskers?" The old man thought about it, and said, "Take my heart, O King, but do not take Lord Mustapha of the long whiskers." – "What do you want for him, then?" said the king. "O King, may you live for ever, I want a ship made half of gold and half of silver, and I want half of all the money in the town." – "It's yours," said the king, "it's yours." So then the old man agreed. The king took the cat, and the old man went away. "Oh," said the king, "we never asked how to feed the cat. Go after the old man and find out!" – "How does he eat?" asked the old man. "Like people!" So the servants sent to inquire came back and said, "He likes people."

Well, they went out of town and brought back a man, but the cat would have nothing to do with him. So they put the cat on a chain, and locked the door of his room. Then they put some beef in front of him, and the cat ate it. They put some bread in front of him, and he ate that too. Next day was Friday. They brought the cat out, to go to the market place with the soldiers. The cat was fastened to the king's girdle, and the king told his guards, "Keep careful watch, in case the cat eats me up." However, the cat was so frightened of the soldiers that he jumped on the king's back. "The cat wants to eat me!" cried the king, and his guards shooed the cat away.

The cat climbed up the tower of the mosque, where the people were busy praying. When the congregation went away, the imam and the hodja remained behind. "What a fine mosque we have!" said the imam. Then he saw the cat at the top of the tower, and said, "If that cat came down now he would eat us up." The hodja saw the cat too. "Come along," said he, "let's escape to another country!" And they ran off in dismay. As for the cat, he went back to the old man.

THE CAT AND THE WOMAN

Long, long ago the cat lived wild in the bush, and not in men's houses. However, he felt lonely, and thought he would join forces with some strong and mighty creature. First he made friends with the hare, and went everywhere with him. But one day the hare quarreled with a stag, who fought and killed him with his horns. So the cat went off with the stag. One day, however, a leopard lying in wait for the stag pounced on him and killed him. The cat thought he would stay with the leopard, but when the leopard was about to eat his fill of the stag's flesh, a lion appeared and drove the leopard away with a couple of blows of his paws. So the cat lived with the lion, thinking that at last he had found the strongest companion of all.

One day, however, the lion and the cat met a herd of elephants. The cat quickly ran up a tree, but the elephants trampled the lion to death. So the cat thought, "Elephants are the biggest and strongest of all animals. I had better make friends with them." He was just wondering how to do it, when a hunter hiding behind a bush shot an elephant with a poisoned arrow. The elephant fell dead, and the rest of the herd ran away in panic and terror. The cat, still up his tree, went on thinking. "That strange creature with two legs doesn't look particularly strong, but all the same he overcame the elephant," he thought. "I must try to make friends with this stranger." So he followed the hunter home, keeping a safe distance between them. The hunter went into his house, and for a while the cat waited timidly outside. Soon he heard terrible shouting and scolding inside the house, the door flew open, and out ran the hunter with a woman after him, beating him with a wooden ladle. Then the cat said, "At last I've found the strongest living creature of all, feared even by the one who killed the elephant! That is the creature I'll live with!" And he went into the kitchen of the house.

THE CAT AND THE LION

The lion had grown old, and so he slept with his mouth open. However, the mice kept getting into his jaws and picking out the bits of meat that were stuck between his teeth, and he could not rest. So he called for a cat, and told her, "Come and stay with me for a few days! Kill those mice, and you can eat them."

The cat came to stay with the lion, and she hadn't a care in the world. There was plenty of good meat to eat whenever she wanted. So the cat thought: this is the life for me, and I'm not giving it up in a hurry. She decided to make her work last longer, and chase the mice away instead of catching and eating them, for it would only take her a couple of days to catch and kill them all. However, she didn't want the lion to know what she was thinking. Every evening, when they ate together, the cat would talk about those mice, and said that although she was killing them, she hadn't caught them all yet. She kept complaining of their numbers. And in this way the cat made herself a comfortable home with the lion.

One day the cat had kittens. She gave her kittens plenty of milk and meat, and they led a carefree life. Time passed by. The kittens grew up, and were now able to look after themselves.

But whenever her kittens wanted to hunt and catch mice, the cat would say, "If you eat all those mice, we'll lose our livelihood. So mind you don't catch and kill them, just give them a scare and let them go." That was her advice to her young.

One day the lion had sent the mother cat off somewhere, and the young and inexperienced kittens, who hadn't been paying attention to what their mother told them, attacked the mice and killed every single one of them within a day or so. When their mother came back from the place where she had been, she saw that there were no mice left, and realized what had happened. Fearing she would have to go away, she went looking for mice everywhere, but there wasn't a mouse to be seen. What was she to do? She gathered her kittens, and when she had explained matters properly, she told them to jump into the lion's jaws while he was asleep and pick out bits of food to eat. However, as one of the kittens was picking out bits of meat from between the lion's teeth, it scratched him with its claws. At that the lion awoke, and leaped up. In answer to his questions, the cat told him, "Some mice got into your mouth, but we've driven them away." But when it

happened a second time, and the lion crushed one of the kittens, the cat began to be afraid. She went around trying to find the mice, and promising them she wouldn't hurt them. However, none of the mice would come.

When the lion realized that there were no mice left, and the cat was trying to deceive him, he drove her away. And as the cat left, she said to the lion, "We'd grown used to each other's company. It was those silly kittens of mine who interfered. Do forgive me if I've done you any wrong, and perhaps we'll meet again."

THE CAT, THE ROOSTER AND THE LAMB

Once upon a time there were two old people who had reared a cat, a rooster and a lamb, and loved them as if they were human. Time went by, and the old man slaughtered a pig he had been fattening up for him and his wife to eat. When the feast day came, the old woman made honey cakes and put the meat on the fire to cook. Now as there was Holy Mass that day, she told the cat to watch the pot of meat while she and her husband went to church. She sent the rooster to fetch water and the lamb to fetch wood. Then the two old people went to church and left the cat watching the pot. When the rooster and the lamb came back they were very hungry, and they saw the cat licking his paws, for he had fished a piece of meat out of the pot and eaten it. Then the rooster asked the cat for some meat from the pot, and so did the lamb. So the cat took some out of the pot and gave them each a little helping. However, when they had eaten what he gave them, the cat said, "Let's eat it all up." So they ate up all the meat the old people had left in the pot to cook. Then the cat said, "I'm going to run away now, or they'll beat me to death for giving you all that meat." – "I'm going too," said the rooster. "So am I," said the lamb.

So the three of them ran away before the old people came home. They came to a mountain with a very tall fir tree growing on it, and a cave beneath the fir tree. The rooster and the cat climbed the tree, and the lamb stayed down below. However, the rooster told the lamb that the two of them would pull him up on a branch. "Hold on to me," said the cat. So the lamb held on to him tight, and the rooster hauled, and they pulled the lamb up on a branch of the tree.

After a while it grew dark, and they heard a noise down in the cave below. Soon after that, the lamb was dying of thirst, and wanted to get a drink of water. "I must, little brothers, I must!" he told the cat and the rooster. "Then climb down very carefully," the cat told him. However, when the lamb tried to climb down, he fell out of the tree. Then a wolf came out of the cave and pounced on the lamb, trying to kill him. But the cat jumped down and dug his claws into the wolf. The wolf ran into his cave again, with the cat after him, scratching him until he was far back in the cave. Then another wolf came up, and the cat scratched that one too. When the wolves ran out of the cave once more, the lamb butted them hard, and the rooster crowed, "Cock-a-doodle-do, can't catch me! Cock-a-doodle-

do, can't catch me!" The wolves ran uphill so fast you could barely see them. Then the cat and the rooster and the lamb moved into the wolves' cave, where they found plenty of meat, so the three of them ate their fill. When the old man and the old woman came home from church, they found neither the cat nor the rooster nor the lamb at home. They didn't know where they might be. But when they saw there was no meat left in the pot, they guessed the animals had eaten it and run away for fear of a beating.

Now the wolves had left a dead stag in their cave, and decided to go and fetch it and take it to the place where they were now living. So they came back when it was dark, and the three friends were sitting up in the fir tree. One wolf went into the cave, saw nobody there, and said to the other, "I don't know where that little man with the four sharp knives has gone. The one with the big head who butted us and knocked us down isn't here either. And there's no sign of the one who cackled so loud." – "Good," said the other wolf, "then let's go in." No sooner were they inside the cave than the cat jumped down from the tree, along with the lamb, and they barred the wolves' way out. Then the cat began scratching them, and whenever they tried to escape the lamb stood in their way, butting them and forcing them back into the cave. As for the rooster, he went on crowing, as he had done before, "Cock-a-doodle-do, can't catch me! Cock-a-doodle-do, can't catch me!" This went on until the cat and the lamb were tired of scratching and butting, and the rooster was tired of crowing, and they let the wolves come out of the cave, half dead by now, and run away. Off they went, and they never came back. So the three animals took the venison the wolves had left there, and went back to the old people. In the evening, when they were nearly home, the cat told the rooster, "You climb up to one window and I'll climb up to the other. And you stand by the door," he told the lamb, "and when I mew, you must butt the door with your head. As for you, you must begin to crow," he said to the rooster.

They did as the cat told them. When the cat mewed, the lamb butted the door with his head and the rooster began to crow. The two old people came out, delighted, crying, "Here are our animals home again! Here they are back!" So they all made merry, and the old folk asked where the animals had been, and the animals told them all that they had done.

THE CAT IN THE MOURNING HAT

There was once a man who had a little cat. He raised this cat and loved her dearly. He let her sit by his table morning and night, and fed her fish and rice. Since the cat was always fed like this, she would come very close to her master's table and wait for him to give her something, and if he ever forgot, she would beg, "Yowng! Yowng!" Then she ate what he gave her, and was very happy.

One day her master suddenly became very sick. He lay in bed for several months, called in doctors from far and wide and swallowed their medicines, but nothing did him any good. He tried all the treatments the most famous of doctors could offer, but they didn't help. His condition was becoming worse and worse.

Then one doctor told him, "There is only one medicine that can cure your sickness, and it would be very hard to get it in a hurry. If you could take this medicine, you would certainly be cured at once. However, as I was saying, it is hard to find." He looked troubled, and you could hear him grind his teeth.

"What is this medicine which you say is so hard to find?" asked the master of the house. "Quick, tell me its name! Speak!" To which the doctor replied, "Well, if you could get a thousand rats, we could make a medicine that would take effect at once." And then he left the house.

The sick man called his family together, and they wondered how they could find a thousand rats. They felt sadder than ever, for they were sure of one thing: if they could not get that medicine, the master of the house would die.

The cat sat there and heard it all. "Good," said she to herself. "At last I have a chance to do something in return for all I've been given. So off she ran. She found herself a mourning hat, came back with it, put the hat on her head, and sat in front of a rat's hole, waiting for the rat to come out.

Before long a rat looked out, and naturally he saw the cat sitting there. So he scuttled straight back into his hole again. He waited impatiently a while, and then put his head cautiously out of the hole once more, to see if the cat was still there. This time the cat saw the rat, and began to scold him. "You wretched creature!" said the cat. "Even a fellow like you, who spends his time hiding in holes underground, ought to be able to see that I'm in mourning. How is it that not one of you rats has been to offer me condolences? Whoever heard of

such a thing! Whoever met such rude, uncivil persons before? Hide as deep in your holes as you like, but I'll summon a host of my friends who will band together, and there will be such a slaughter among you that not one of you will be left alive!" Terrified, the rat ran back into his hole, and gathered all the other rats together. The first to speak was a dignified old rat, who said, "Listen to me! Bad as that cat may be, she's in mourning, so she will hardly do us any harm. But if we're not careful, who knows how this may end? Unhappily for us, I am afraid! I will go out first, and express my sympathy to the cat, and see how she takes it. Then we will meet again, and I'll tell you how things stand." The cat was sitting outside the rat's hole, as before, with the mourning hat on her head. She did not look as if she were planning to pounce on the rat, so the rat summoned up all his courage, stepped out, made a bow, and offered condolences in a suitable manner. "Living in a poor way as I do, I didn't know that you were in mourning," he said, "and that's why I did not make haste to express my sympathy. It really was unpardonable! I bow to you a hundred times and beg you to forgive me." And he groveled on the ground. The cat received his expressions of sympathy in a friendly manner, much to the rat's relief, and he hurried back down the hole and told the others, "There's nothing to worry about. Go up, quick, offer your condolences and then come back!" So rat after rat went up and bowed low, which seemed to please the cat. However, suddenly the cat said, "So many of you have come that it is hard to thank each of you separately for your sympathy. We must find some other way. I wonder... perhaps it sounds uncivil, but could you not all assemble in the great square, with your entire families? Then I could receive your expressions of sympathy all at once. How would that be? At what time and on what day would you care to gather together?"

The rats themselves thought this a much more convenient plan, and they agreed at once, and told all the other rats.

So on the appointed day, rats came from all directions and gathered in the great square, and stood there thronging close together.

But the cat had summoned all her friends, and they were lying in wait where nobody could see them. When the rats had all assembled, and were only waiting for the cat, she appeared with the mourning hat on her head, as if to receive the rats' condolences, looking most dignified. But then the other cats leaped out of hiding, and began to kill the rats. Within a very short time a couple of thousand rats lay dead. The cat in the mourning hat ran home and fastened her teeth into the garments of the very first member of the household she met. The man thought this was a very strange thing, but he followed the cat, and saw thousands of rats, ready to be collected.

How happy the master of the house was! The doctor was called, and made the medicine from the rats – and the sick man was completely cured. And so the cunning cat paid back her master for all his kindness.

THE MOUSE AND THE CAT

There was once a mouse who lived near a village, and one day it got into the larder of a farmer's house. But when the cat was aware of that mouse she went after it and chased it.

The mouse ran for its life as fast as ever it could. It scurried out of the village, making for its hole, where it would be safe. However, before it could slip down the hole the cat caught up, seized it by the tail, and the tail came off.

The mouse ran down its hole, scared and tailless, and licked its wounds.

The cat sat outside, licking at the mouse's tail with pleasure, and wondering how to entice the mouse out again. She mewed very sweetly, and said, "Dear mouse, I only wanted to play! But you were so hasty, and ran away too fast, and so your tail broke off. Do come out! I would so like to talk to you!"

However, the mouse knew the cat's cunning way with words, and said, "Oh no, you only want to eat me. I'm not coming out of my hole, not I!"

So the cat mewed sweetly, and said, "Oh, but I only want to play with you, so please come out!"

However, when all her persuasions failed, the cat said, "Dear mouse, I still have your tail here. Wouldn't you like it back? I can stick it on behind you again."

"Very kind of you, I'm sure, my dear cat," said the mouse. "But I'd rather live my life without a tail than end up inside you with one!"

CONTENTS